About the Book

Through the centuries, the story of Androcles and the lion has fascinated boys and girls in every age.

Quail Hawkins' simple retelling from Apion of this favorite retains the drama and flavor of the original version. It captures the bustle and excitement of an ancient city, the hardships of slave life, the might of the Colosseum, and, most important, the warmth and loyalty between man and beast.

Distinguished woodcuts by Rocco Negri add a new dimension to a classic story. Bold, vivid line and color convey and accentuate the atmosphere of long ago.

COWARD-McCANN, INC.   NEW YORK

Androcles and the Lion

Retold from Apion
by Quail Hawkins

Illustrated by Rocco Negri

Second Impression

SBN: GB 698-30012-2

Library of Congress Catalog Card Number: 75-104301

Printed in the United States of America

T 49120

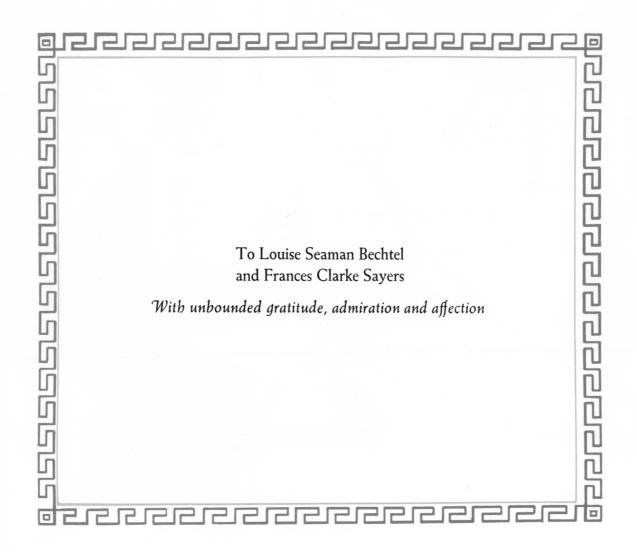

To Louise Seaman Bechtel
and Frances Clarke Sayers

With unbounded gratitude, admiration and affection

Once, many years ago, when the great city of Rome ruled the world, there was in Egypt a slave named Androcles.

Androcles lived in the house of a cruel master. Each day he beat Androcles, and each day he gave him barely enough food to keep him alive.

At last Androcles could bear it no longer. He knew he must run away. If he were caught, he would be put to death. "Alas," he said to himself, "it would be better to be dead than to live like this." And from that day on, Androcles waited for the time to escape.

One day, amid clouds of dust, the noisy shouts of the camel boys, and the thud of camel hooves, a large caravan passed through the town. Androcles saw his chance. He ran along with the stragglers behind the caravan as if he were part of it. Soon he was safely out of the town and away from his master. But still Androcles was afraid. Every time anyone spoke to him he feared he would be recognized as a runaway slave.

When the caravan reached the wilderness, grass and tall thick thorn trees lined the narrow trail. There, driven by his fear, Androcles slipped into a patch of high grass and waited until the caravan was out of sight. Now Androcles was indeed a free man, but a starving one.

Weak with hunger and parched with thirst, he started out wearily in search of water. When he could go no farther, he collapsed in the shade of a thorn tree to rest.

Suddenly a terrifying roar brought Androcles to his feet. Not far
away lay a huge lion, a great tawny beast with a thick, blackish mane.
Androcles stood shaking with fright. He was too afraid to move, and
he knew the lion would attack him before he could escape.

But the beast did not seem to notice Androcles. He was licking and biting at one of his forepaws as if it had been hurt.

Androcles was now less afraid than astonished. He came slowly toward the lion until he saw a large thorn embedded in his paw. Androcles crept nearer and nearer, speaking softly. Timidly he put out his hand to touch the lion's paw. The lion seemed to sense Androcles would not hurt him. He let Androcles pick up the injured paw, grasp the end of the thorn, and with a quick jerk pull it out. The lion roared with pain, but settled back to lick his paw again. He looked up at Androcles and licked his hand.

Androcles lost all fear of the great beast and gently stroked the huge head. Suddenly the lion stood up. Androcles saw that the lion wished to be followed. Androcles walked behind until they came to a thicket near a large water hole. Gratefully Androcles dropped to the edge of the pool, and he and the lion both drank thirstily.

After drinking, the lion left Androcles, who hid himself in a thicket and wondered what to do next. He was no longer thirsty, but he was still hungry. He was thankful that the lion had brought him to water, but now the lion had gone.

Androcles did not wonder long, for soon the lion returned dragging a small gazelle. He dropped it beside Androcles, who was overjoyed to see food. He drew his knife, the only tool he had, and shared the meat with the lion. Androcles made a fire and roasted his portion. Together they ate and slept.

With water close by and food enough for both they became good companions. The grateful lion fed Androcles the same way each day, and each day Androcles felt less and less afraid. Sometimes he even forgot he was an escaped slave and walked like a free man.

Alas, one day his happiness was abruptly ended. While he and the lion napped during the heat of the day, hunters crept up on them and captured them.

Androcles was turned in to the authorities as a runaway slave
and the hunters collected their reward. Androcles did not know
what they did with the lion.

Now it was the custom in those days for criminals, such as escaped slaves or Christians, to be punished by being put into a large arena with wild beasts that had been kept without food until they were very hungry and savage. They would tear the poor prisoners apart while crowds of people watched. These events called circuses were held in large amphitheaters in different parts of the empire. The largest one, called the Colosseum, was in Rome. When Androcles was dragged before the authorities, they decreed that he should be sent to Rome to die.

In Rome, Androcles knew that he was doomed. He could never escape again. "You are lucky that you were not put to death in Egypt," his guards told him. "Now you will have the honor to die before the emperor and all his court. Besides, you still have a chance for life. If you are exceptionally brave, the emperor can, if he wishes, spare your life."

Androcles did not feel brave and could not imagine that the great emperor of Rome would notice him, a hopeless slave. He wept for his brief time of freedom and his one friend, the lion.

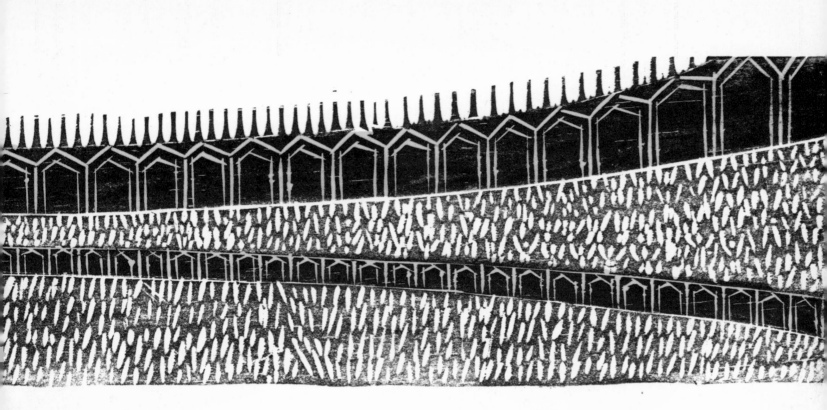

The day came for the terrible circus. Huge crowds filled the Colosseum, that great stadium with its enormous arena in the center. In splendor the emperor of all Rome entered to sounds of music and shouts from the admiring crowd.

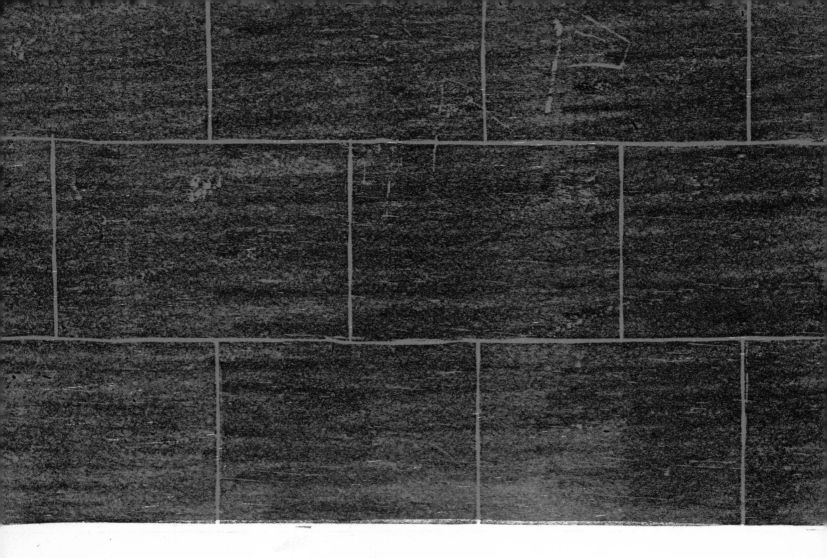

Waiting behind barred gates down in the arena, Androcles could see the emperor sitting in a box at the most favorable spot to view the sports—close enough to see everything, but safe from dangerous beasts.

At last the time came for Androcles to enter the arena to meet his death. He walked in fearfully, armed with only a cudgel. For a moment Androcles could see nothing. Across the arena a gate was opened and a great lion came out, his tail switching angrily as he saw Androcles. Androcles stopped. He had no place to run, no place to hide. Closer and closer bounded the angry lion.

Suddenly the great beast stopped. He stared at Androcles for a long, terrifying minute. As Androcles stood wondering, the lion came gamboling toward him like a playful kitten. When he reached Androcles, instead of tearing him with his great claws, the lion nearly knocked Androcles down, smelling him and licking his face and hands. Androcles recognized his friend, the grateful lion. He put his arms around the lion's neck and stroked him tenderly as he had before when they had eaten together in the wilderness.

A ripple of surprise ran through the watching crowd. There stood the man and the hungry lion, peacefully! The people could not believe it! Neither could the guards, but they came forward to kill the slave because the lion would not.

Suddenly the emperor stood up, his arms outstretched. His hands were clenched into fists. A roar of approval came from the crowd as they, too, stood up with their closed fists outstretched. The guards lowered their spears.

The emperor spoke: "Have that man brought before us."

Androcles walked slowly toward the emperor's box. What would happen to him now? The crowd continued to scream! Then Androcles saw the lion walking at his side. He put his hand gently on the lion's mane and looked up into the eyes of the most powerful man on earth.

He looked down on them—the slave and the lion—and, glancing somewhat uneasily at the lion, said, "Is that beast safe?"

"As long as I am here, Your Highness." Androcles smiled.

The emperor smiled, too. "Now tell us why this fierce lion did not tear you apart and feast on your flesh?"

Androcles told the emperor how he had run away and had made friends with the grateful lion.

"Such gratitude must be rewarded," spoke the emperor. "You shall both go free!"

And so it was!

The Author

QUAIL HAWKINS was born in Spokane, Washington, where she was the oldest of seven children. She was the only girl among the seven. From an early age, her "chore" was telling stories to the others. She was an avid reader, and upon graduation, she went into the retail children's book field. For a time, she worked in children's book publishing in New York City, but eventually she returned to California, where she became a buyer of children's books. She is presently the library consultant for schools and libraries for the Sather Gate Book Shop.

In addition to her work in the field of children's books, Miss Hawkins is the author of many books for boys and girls, and she has taught creative writing and children's literature.

The Artist

ROCCO NEGRI has illustrated a number of books for young people. He has studied at the Art Students League of New York and at the School of Visual Arts. Mr. Negri lives in Ridgewood, New York with his wife and two children.